For Alice and Melissa (Laura)

First U.S. edition 1993
First published in Great Britain in 1992
by Walker Books Ltd., London.

Library of Congress Cataloging-in-Publication Data:

Dale, Penny.
All about Alice / Penny Dale. —1st U.S. ed.
Summary: Alice has a busy day playing while her big sister is in school.
[1. Play—Fiction.]   I. Title.
PZ7 . D1525A1   1992   [E]—dc20   92-52991
ISBN 1-56402-171-8 (lib. bdg.)

10 9 8 7 6 5 4 3 2 1

Printed in Hong Kong

The artwork for this book was done in
watercolor and colored pencil.

Candlewick Press
2067 Massachusetts Avenue
Cambridge, Massachusetts 02140

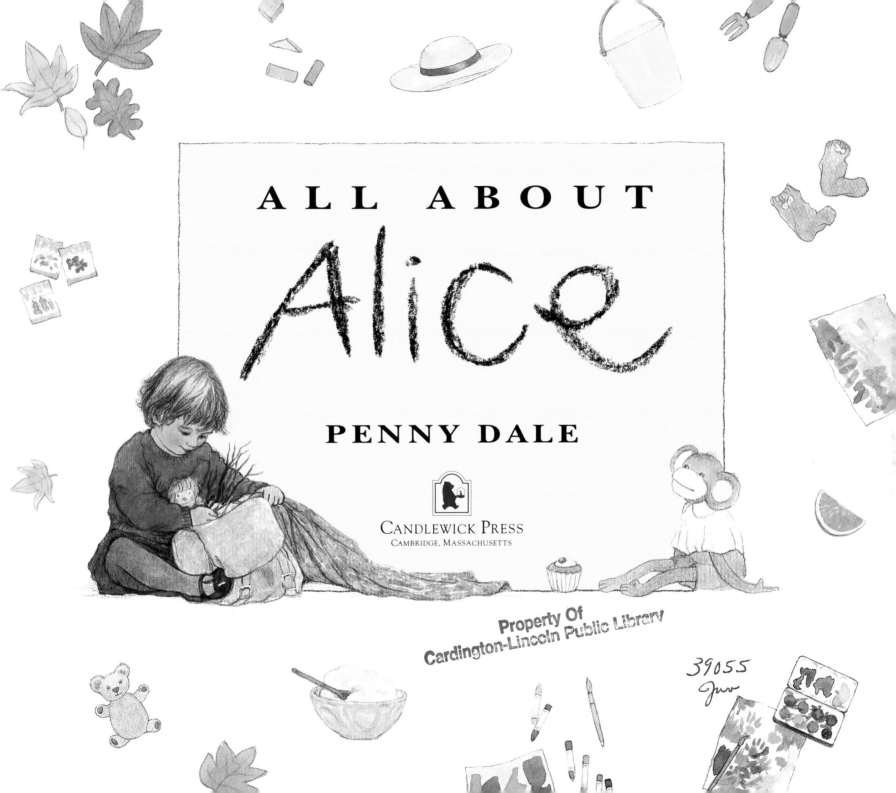

ALL ABOUT
Alice

PENNY DALE

CANDLEWICK PRESS
CAMBRIDGE, MASSACHUSETTS

Alice was getting dressed. So was her big sister Laura.

wool sweater

sweater with a face on it

hat with ducks on it

green pants

socks

overalls

knee socks

pleated skirt

Here are some of
Alice's clothes.

What do you think
she put on?

shiny shoes

blue bloomers

underwear

party dress

red coat

green tights

frilly socks

blue skirt

itchy sweater

Laura's old schoolbag

bear T-shirt

Alice put on her sweater with a face on it, her green pants, her blue skirt,
her hat with ducks on it, and Laura's old schoolbag.

Then Dad came in and helped her dress right and took her down to breakfast.

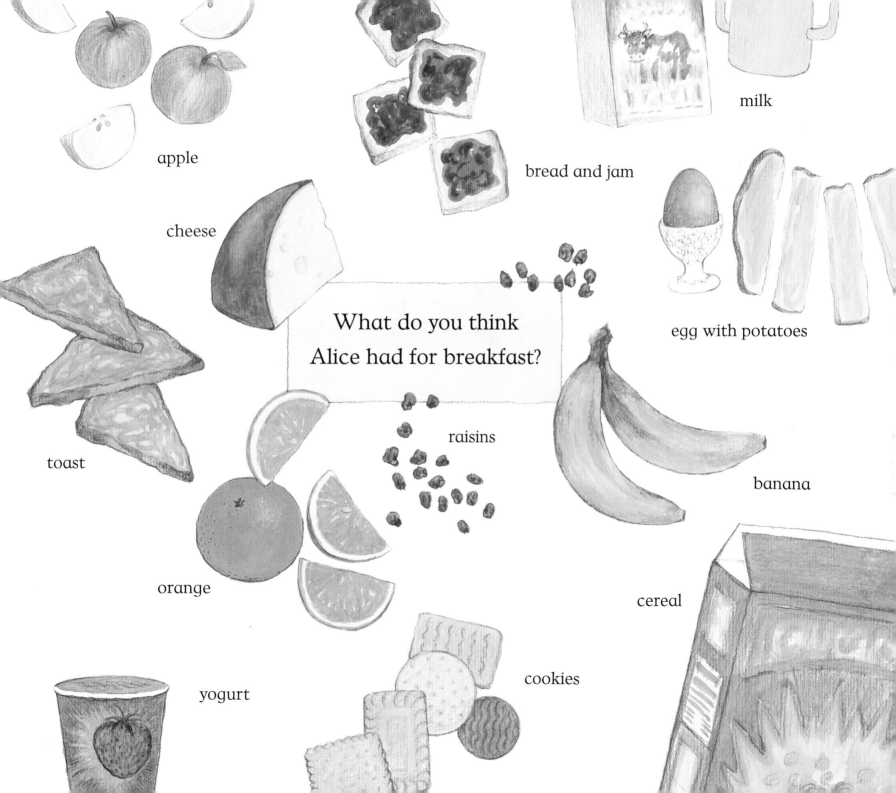

apple

bread and jam

milk

cheese

egg with potatoes

What do you think
Alice had for breakfast?

toast

raisins

banana

orange

cereal

yogurt

cookies

Alice had cereal for breakfast, but she didn't eat it.

Alice wanted her sister's breakfast.

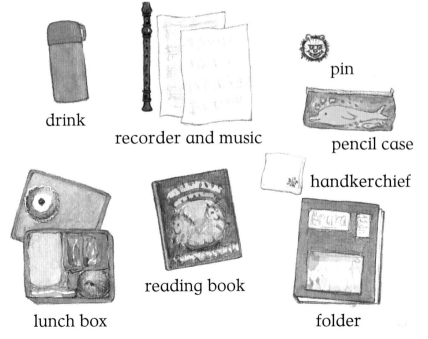

drink

recorder and music

pin

pencil case

handkerchief

lunch box

reading book

folder

After breakfast Laura packed her schoolbag. This is what she put in it.

crayons

old raisins

leaves

Laura's cupcake

scarf

crumpled paper

Alice packed her
schoolbag too.

What do you think
she put in it?

car

jewels

pink recorder

crusts

monkey

some cereal

book

rock

twigs

old candy

Alice put everything into her schoolbag, except her monkey and her sister's cupcake.

She carried her monkey and gave back the cupcake.

Mom, Alice, and Laura walked to school.

On the playground Alice started to cry. Why do you think Alice cried?

Alice cried because Laura and the other big children went into school without her.
She was too young to go to school.

Mom and Alice walked home.

driving the tractor

playing in the garden

reading

making a house

These are some of the things that Alice likes doing at home.

When she got home, what do you think Alice did?

playing school

playing with blocks

painting

cooking

helping with the dishes

At home Alice went straight upstairs to play school.

She went out into the garden and found a spider.

She did some painting and cooking and reading. She helped with the dishes.

one sandwich

one small tomato

three pieces of cheese

half a yogurt

twenty-seven chips

four slices of cucumber

one big apple

a cupcake like Laura's

At lunchtime Alice had a picnic in the garden. This is what she ate.

After lunch Alice made a house and drove the tractor around the garden.

She went back upstairs to play school, and then it was time for a nap.

bird

rabbit

koala

mouse

Who do you think
Alice had a nap with?

little teddy

big teddy

monkey

fox

Alice napped with all of the animals.

Mom woke Alice when it was time to pick up Laura from school. Alice was

grumpy at first.   But soon she was smiling again. Why do you think she was smiling?

Alice was smiling because she knew that Laura and
the other big children were about to come out of school.

In the schoolyard, Alice played with Amy and the twins. Then it was time to go home.

Can you see Laura?

What do you think Alice did all the way home?

All the way home Alice copied her big sister.

When they got home Alice went on copying her sister.
She copied her playing the recorder. She copied her watching TV.

She copied her going upstairs. What do you think happened
when Laura went into their room?

When Laura went into their room, she was angry with Alice because of the mess. She said she wanted to play alone and picked up her things.

Alice played alone too. But she didn't pick up her things, she got more out.

tie-on wings

dressing-up clothes

Here are the things
Alice got out.

What do you think
happened next?

old decorations

masks

face paints

hats

Alice got dressed up. Then the twins and Amy came over.

Everyone got dressed up like Alice—even Laura—

and they all ran out into the garden to play.